CW00742378

A Templar Book

Produced by The Templar Company plc,
Pippbrook Mill, London Road, Dorking, Surrey RH4 1JE, Great Britain.

Text copyright © *The Fairies' Christmas Party* 1926-1953 by Darrell Waters Limited
Illustration and design copyright © 1993 by The Templar Company plc
Enid Blyton is a registered trademark of Darrell Waters Limited

This edition produced for Parragon Books,
Unit A, Central Trading Estate, Bath Road, Brislington, Bristol.

This book contains material first published as
Peggy's Musical Box in Enid Blyton's Sunny Stories
and Sunny Stories between 1926 and 1953.

Illustrated by Alison Winfield

Printed and bound in Italy

ISBN 1 85813 334 3

Enid Blyton's

THE FAIRIES' CHRISTMAS PARTY

Illustrated by Alison Winfield

PARRAGON

Emma's toys all lived in a big wooden cupboard in the playroom. There were four dolls, a teddy bear, a big panda, an elephant, two bunnies, a jack-in-the-box, a postman and a dog. There was a box of wooden bricks, a dolls' house, a tea-set and a lovely musical box that Emma had been given for her birthday.

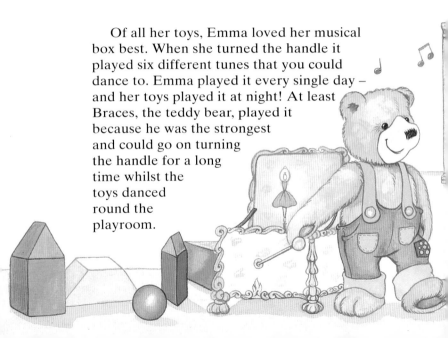

Of all her toys, Emma loved her musical box best. When she turned the handle it played six different tunes that you could dance to. Emma played it every single day – and her toys played it at night! At least Braces, the teddy bear, played it because he was the strongest and could go on turning the handle for a long time whilst the toys danced round the playroom.

One cold, frosty night, a pixie
flew to the window and looked in.
She saw the toys dancing, while
Braces turned the handle on
the musical box. She thought
it was a lovely sight, so she
jumped down from the
window-sill, took hold
of the panda and
danced round
the playroom
with him.

After that she often came
to the playroom to listen
to the musical box and to
join in the dancing.
It was great fun.

"I shan't be coming tomorrow night," she told them one evening. "It is Christmas Eve and the Fairy Queen is holding a dance at the bottom of the garden. We are going to have a band from Dreamland to play for us – a wonderful band that can play dance music better than any other band in the world!"

"We'll peep out of the window and see if we can hear it," promised Braces.

So, on Christmas Eve, the toys all leaned out of the window to hear the band – but although they listened and listened they couldn't hear a thing!

They were wondering
what could have
happened, when the
little pixie came flying
up to the window
quite out
of breath.

"Oh dear," she said, "what *do* you think has happened? Why, the Dreamland band has made a mistake. They thought the Queen's dance was tomorrow, instead of tonight – and they haven't come!"

"What are you going to do?" asked the teddy bear. "Have all the guests arrived?"

"Yes, all of them!" said the pixie. "And there is no music for them to dance to. Isn't it dreadful?"

"Dreadful!" agreed the toys, shaking their heads. But what could be done?

Then the teddy bear
had a marvellous idea.
"I say!" he cried.
"What about the
musical box? You
could dance to
that, and I
could come
and turn
the handle
for you!"

"Ooh! What a good idea!" cried the pixie, delighted. "The Queen will be so pleased, and all the guests will think the musical box is wonderful!"

"Well, we will have to ask Emma first if she will lend it to us," said Braces to the pixie. "You see, the musical box belongs to her, and she is very fond of it. I am sure it isn't right to borrow things belonging to other people unless you ask them first. Shall I go and ask her?"

"Let's all go!" said the big panda.

So the toys crept along the darkened hallway, up the stairs and into the bedroom where Emma lay fast asleep, dreaming dreams of Christmas.

Braces hopped up on to the bed and shook her gently. She awoke with surprise and sat up, rubbing her eyes.

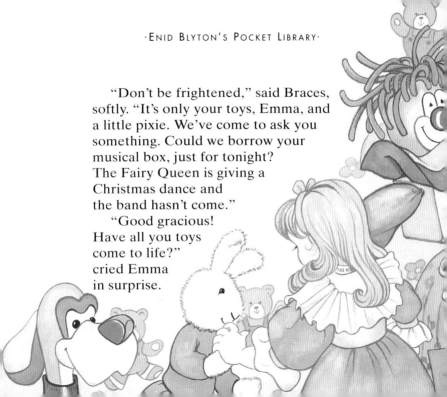

"Don't be frightened," said Braces, softly. "It's only your toys, Emma, and a little pixie. We've come to ask you something. Could we borrow your musical box, just for tonight? The Fairy Queen is giving a Christmas dance and the band hasn't come."

"Good gracious! Have all you toys come to life?" cried Emma in surprise.

"Sshh! Don't wake the grown-ups," said Braces. "Yes, we toys always come to life at night, Emma. But what about your beautiful musical box? *Please* may we borrow it? Just for tonight."

"Of course!" said Emma. "I would be delighted to lend it for a fairy dance – but who will turn the handle?"

"I will," said Braces. "I always turn the handle because my arms are strong and they don't get tired."

"What fun!" said Emma. "Oh, look at this dear little pixie! Are you real?"

"Of course I am!" said the pixie, laughing.

"Thank you *so* much for lending us the musical box. We promise to take great care of it."

They ran out of the bedroom, leaving Emma to fall asleep again, this time dreaming of pixies and teddy bears that could walk and talk.

"Who will carry the musical box?" asked Panda when they were all back in the playroom. "It is very heavy!"

The toys thought about it for a moment and then Braces decided to ask the strong wooden horse if he could manage to carry it in his cart down to the end of the garden. He said he could, so off they all went, out through the playroom window.

It was cold out in the garden and a fluffy layer of snow covered the grass. The light from a silvery moon and a thousand twinkling stars lit their way and made the garden look so beautiful that the toys thought they had reached Fairyland.

Very soon they arrived at the place where the dance was supposed to be, under the shelter of a big fir tree. The Fairy Queen was there, looking very disappointed, and all the guests were wondering what to do.

They were most surprised to see the toys but the little pixie lost no time in explaining why they had come.

The Queen was delighted to hear about the musical box. Then, Braces and the big panda lifted it out of the cart and Braces started to turn the handle.

The tinkling music began and soon all the fairy folk were dancing merrily, round and round beneath the branches of the old tree. All the toys danced too, and Panda even danced with the Fairy Queen herself!

At midnight, everyone sat down and had a delicious feast. There were fairy cakes, cups of tasty nectar and soft sweets made from honey. The toys wanted the party to go on for ever. They had never had such a good time in all their lives!

When the first light of dawn tinged the sky, the fairies said it was time for them to leave. The toys knew that they too should go – back to the playroom, for it would soon be daylight.

"Well, thank you very much indeed," said the Fairy Queen. "Your musical box certainly made our Christmas party a great success. It was so kind of you to lend it to me."

"Oh, Emma lent it, we didn't," said Braces, and he told the Queen all about the little girl and how they had woken her up to ask about the musical box. "She is really very kind and good to us," he said.

"Well, it was very kind of her," said the Fairy Queen. "I must send a letter to thank her." And, taking out a tiny sheet of paper and a beautiful silver pen, she wrote a little letter and tucked it under Brace's belt. She said goodbye and wished them all a Merry Christmas. Then she drove away in her golden carriage with the Fairy King by her side.

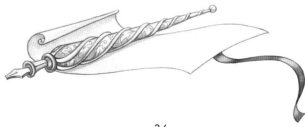

The toys stood and waved until the Queen's carriage had disappeared in the distance. All the fairies, except for the little pixie, had left with her.

"I must go, too," said the pixie. "And you must go home. Thank you so much for helping us." And with that she flew away, after the Fairy Queen.

"Merry Christmas!" cried the toys after her. "Come and see us again soon!"

When Emma woke up she quite forgot at first that it was Christmas Day. All she could think about was how her toys had come to life the night before.

She ran to the playroom to ask
them about it – but
they were all sitting
very still and quiet.
They could not
speak or move
because now
it was
daytime.

Emma began to wonder if it had all been a dream. She went back to her bedroom and looked in her Christmas stocking – and what do you think she found? Right on top of all her presents was a tiny letter, written in the most perfect handwriting! Emma pulled it out and opened it – it said:

Dear Emma,
    Thank you very much
for lending us your lovely
musical box. Will you
please come to our next
dance, when the moon is
full, and bring your
musical box again? The
Fairy King says he would
love to dance with you.
    Have a very Merry
Christmas.
    Love from
        The Fairy Queen

Well, Emma could hardly believe her eyes! Would she go? Of course she would, and the moon will soon be full again so she won't have to wait too long, will she?